Farmer Green...

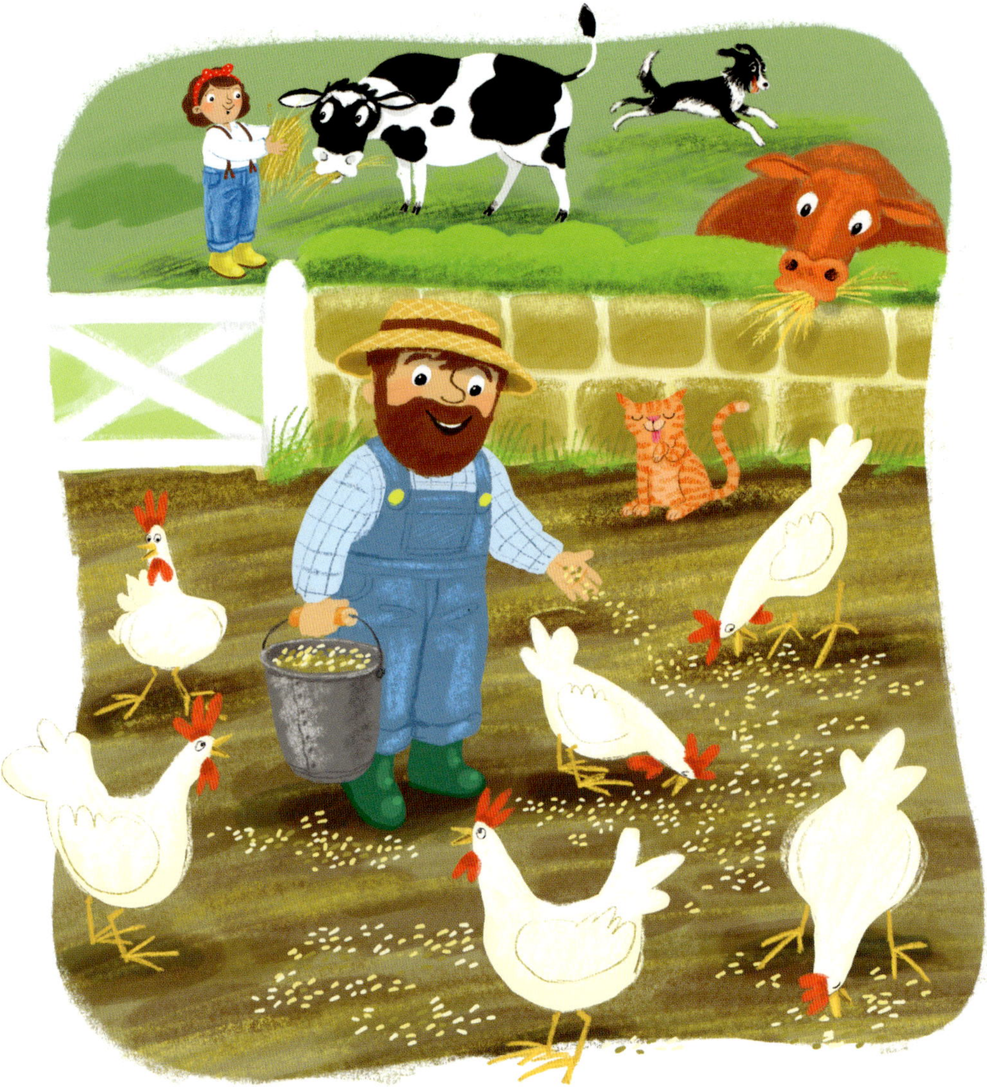

feeds the hens,

collects the eggs

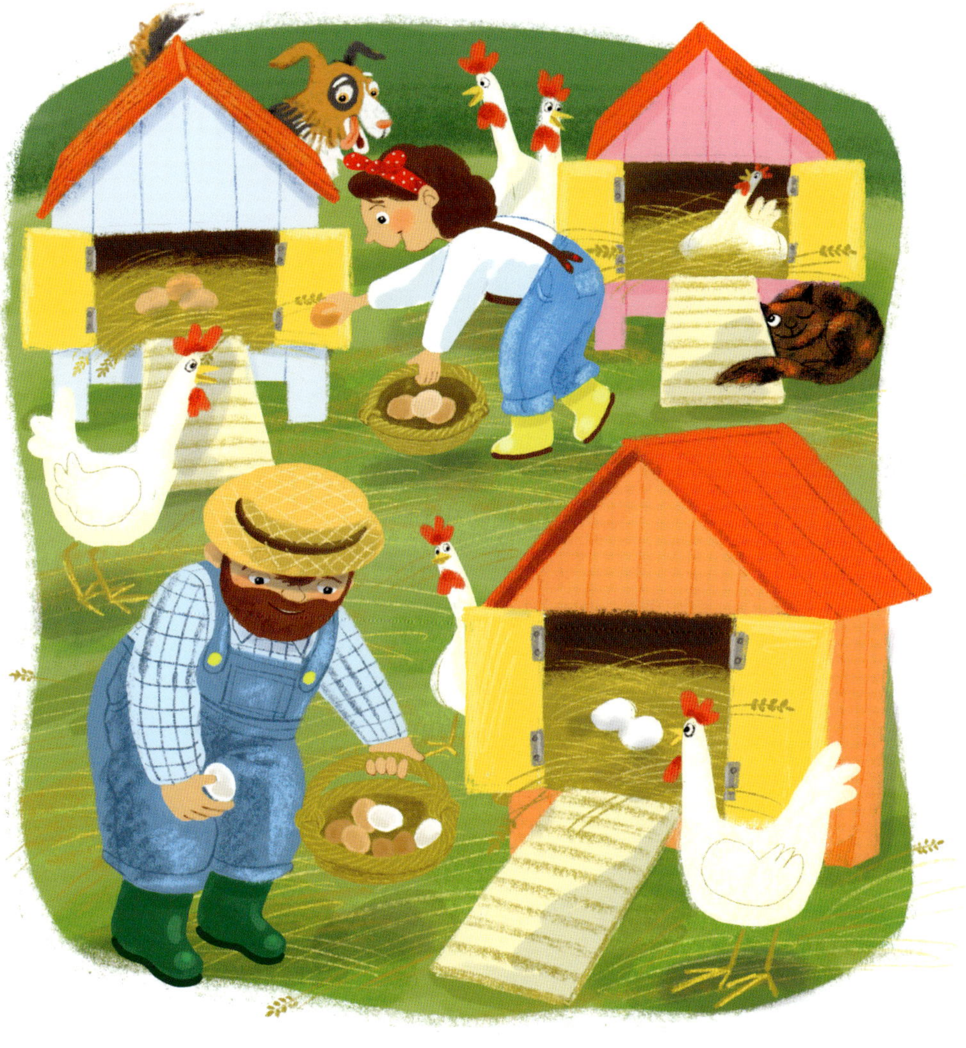

and counts the sheep.

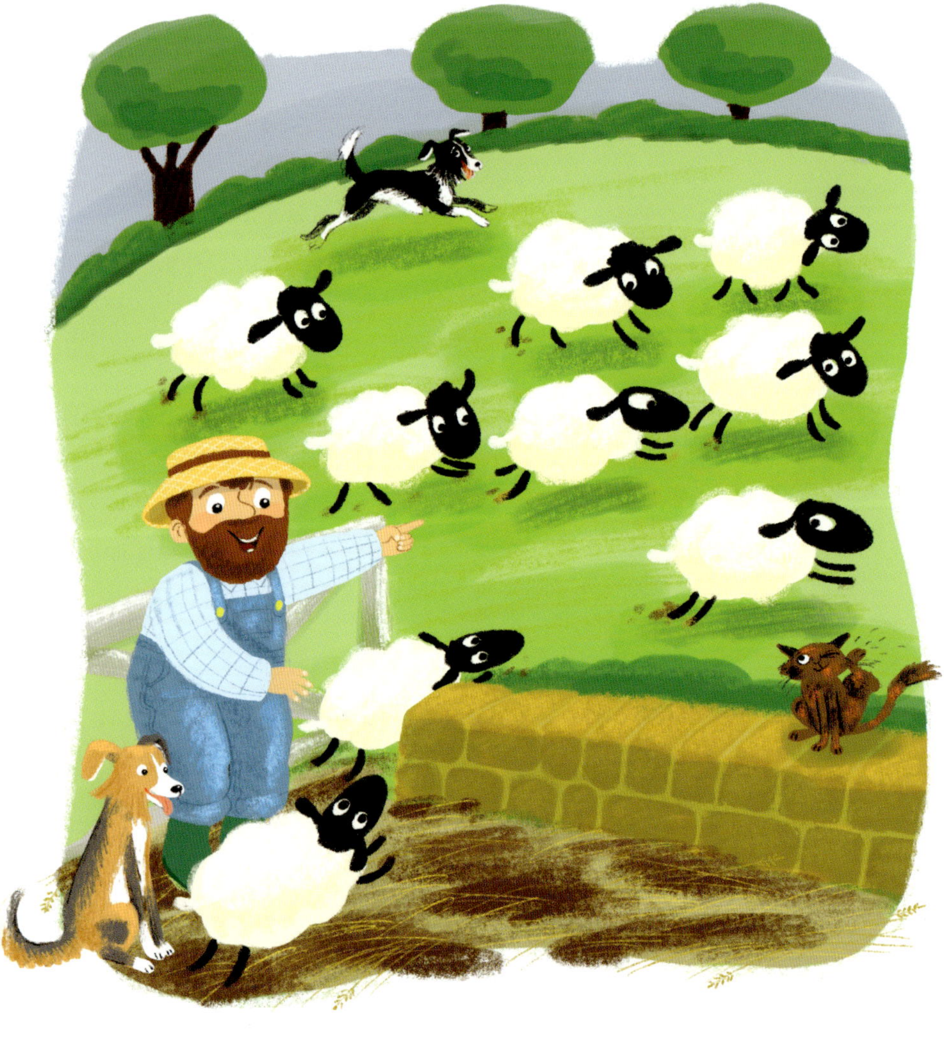

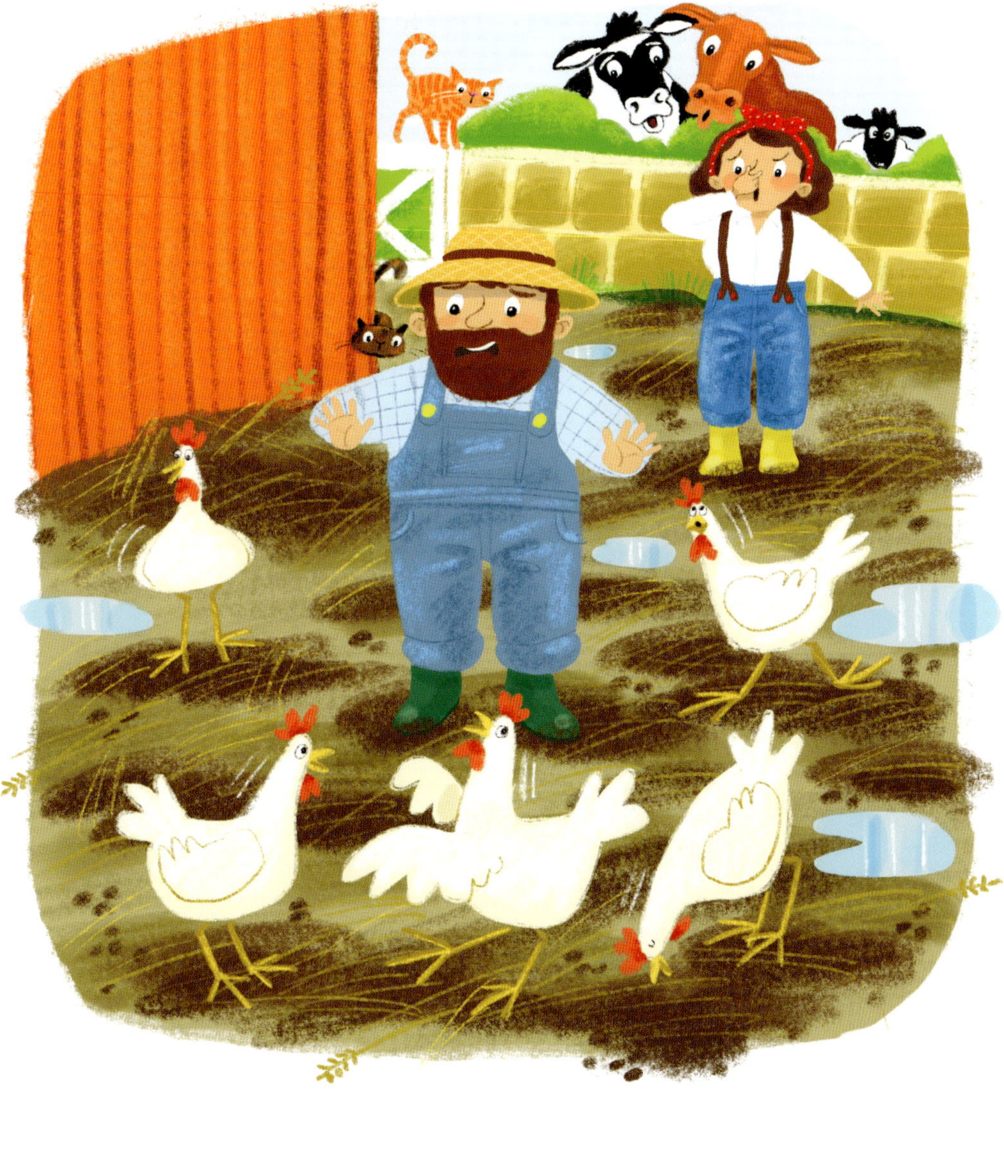

"Yuck!"

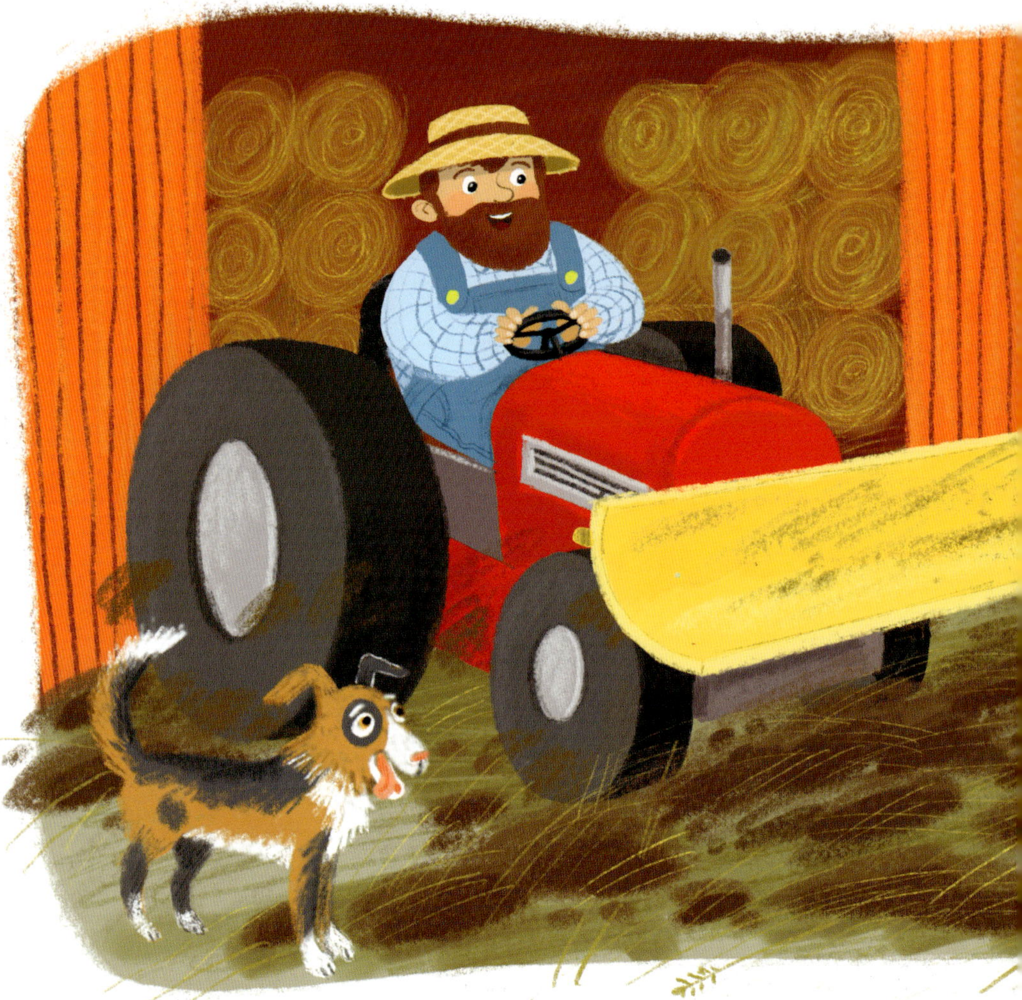

Then, with

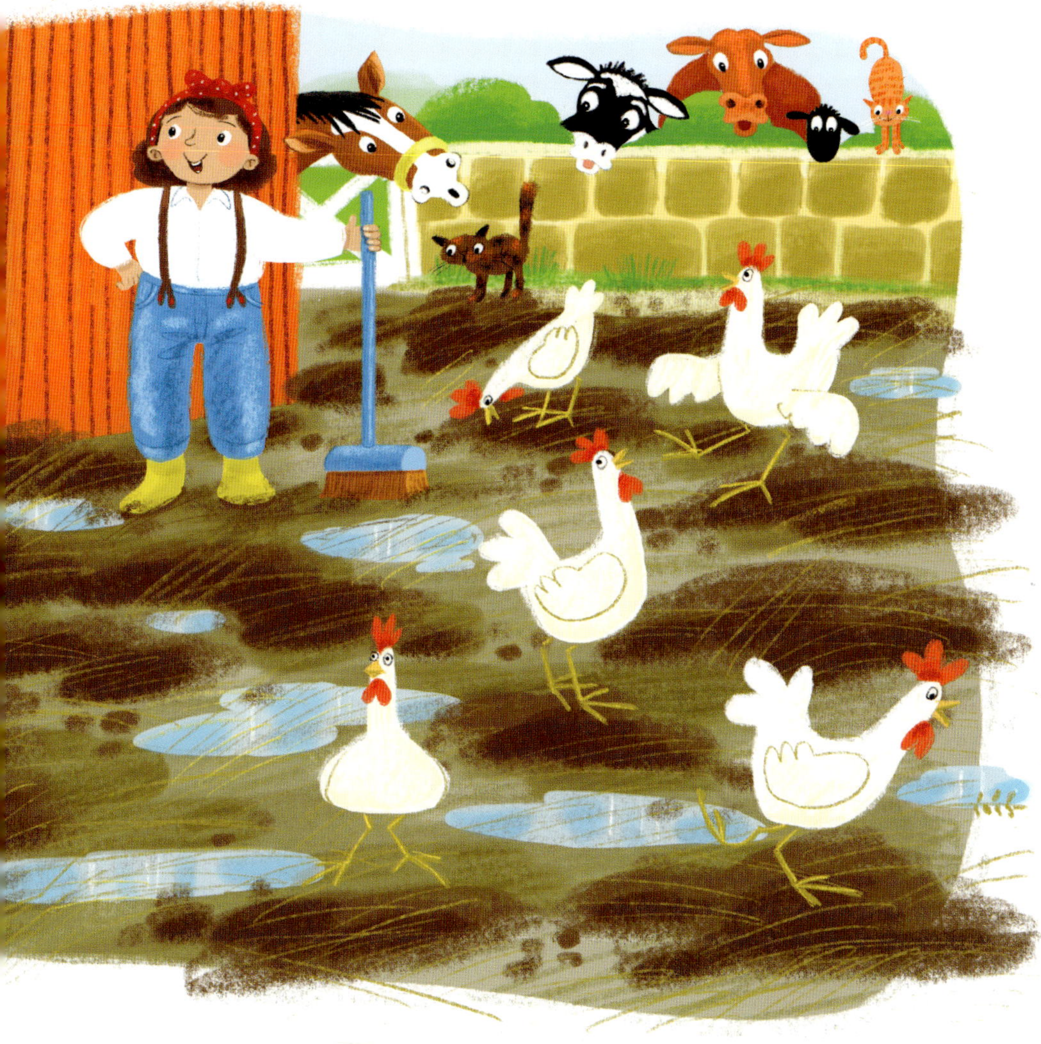

the tractor...

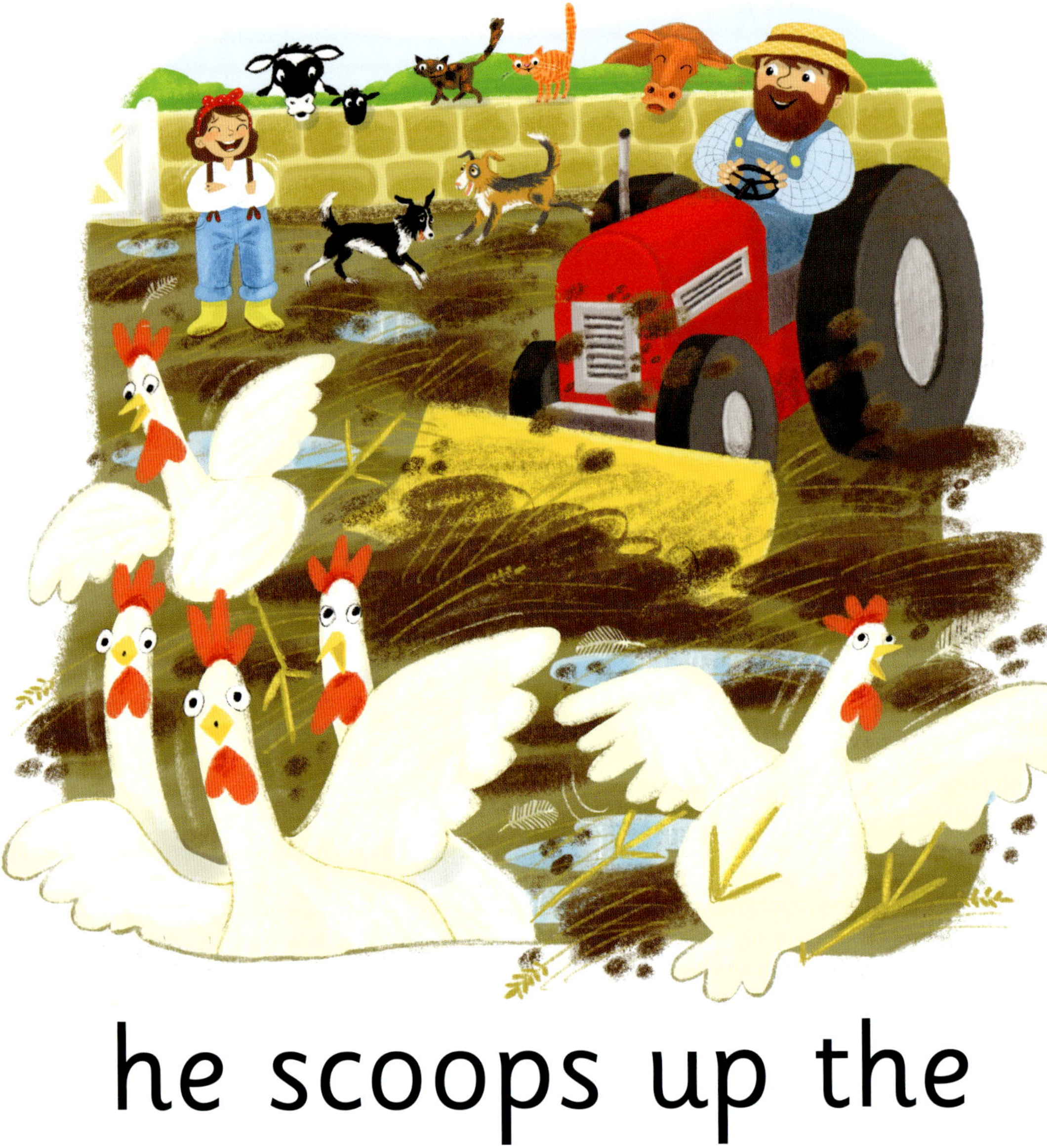

he scoops up the muck!